HELLO! WELCOME TO THE FABUMOUSE WORLD OF THE THEA SISTERS!

P9-CQQ-348

Thea Sisters

Hi, I'm Thea Stilton, Geronimo Stilton's sister! I am a special reporter for _The Rodent's Gazette_, the most famous newspaper on Mouse Island. I love traveling and meeting new mice all over the world, like the Thea Sisters. These five friends have helped me out with my adventures. Let me introduce you to these fabumouse young mice!

Colette has a real passion for fashion. She loves to design her own clothes in her favorite color, pink.

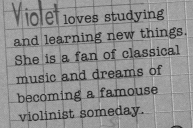

Violet loves studying and learning new things. She is a fan of classical music and dreams of becoming a famous violinist someday.

Pamela loves pizza so much she eats it for breakfast. She is a skilled mechanic who can fix just about any motor she gets her paws on.

PAULINA is shy and loves to read about faraway places. But she loves traveling to those places even more.

Nicky is from the Australian outback, where she developed a love of nature and the environment. This outdoors-loving mouse is always on the move.

The a Sisters

Thea Stilton

MOUSEFORD ACADEMY

DRAMA AT MOUSEFORD

Scholastic Inc.

ISBN 978-0-545-64532-4

Copyright © 2009 by Edizioni Piemme S.p.A., Corso Como 15, 20154 Milan, Italy.

International Rights © Atlantyca S.p.A.

English translation © 2014 by Atlantyca S.p.A.

Based on an original idea by Elisabetta Dami.

www.geronimostilton.com

Published by Scholastic Inc., 557 Broadway, New York, NY 10012.
SCHOLASTIC and associated logos are trademarks and/or registered trademarks of Scholastic Inc.

Stilton is the name of a famous English cheese. It is a registered trademark of the Stilton Cheese Makers' Association. For more information, go to www.stiltoncheese.com.

Text by Thea Stilton
Original title *L'amore va in scena a Topford!*
Cover by Giuseppe Facciotto
Illustrations by Giuseppe Facciotto (pencils) and Davide Turotti (color)
Graphics by Yuko Egusa

Special thanks to Tracey West
Translated by Julia Heim
Interior design by Theresa Venezia

14 13 12   19   20/0

Printed in the U.S.A.   40
First printing, January 2014

HAPPY BIRTHDAY, MOUSEFORD!

The air at MOUSEFORD ACADEMY was filled with excitement. The school was turning SIX HUNDRED YEARS old!

A big birthday like that called for a big CELEBRATION. The professors at the academy had been trying for weeks to come up with the *perfect* event to mark the occasion.

The school's headmaster, Professor Octavius de Mousus, PAWED through the pages of ideas. But he just couldn't make up his mind. There were SO many to choose from!

A **CHEESE** festival? A cheese-sculpting contest? Fireworks? Nothing seemed quite perfect enough. He just couldn't decide.

An important Decision

The Thea Sisters could all feel the **excitement** in the air. They felt lucky to be at the school during such an important anniversary.

"**WOW**, can you believe this place has been here for six hundred years?" Nicky asked.

"I can't wait to find out what the big celebration will be," Pamela said. "I hope it's a **SUPER-CHEESY** feast!"

"Oooh, or a really big dance!"

Colette exclaimed, clapping her paws.

"I was thinking that a concert would be nice," Violet added.

"Whatever it is, I'm sure it will be *mousetastic*," Paulina said confidently. "The professors are working really hard on this."

Pam suddenly looked alarmed. "Hey! You don't think they'll do a math marathon or a spelling bee, do you?"

Her friends all burst out laughing.

"I hope not," Paulina answered. "I'm sure whatever they're planning will be FUN."

Nicky frowned. "Unless the Ruby Crew decides to spoil things, like they usually do."

The Thea Sisters all knew what Nicky meant. **Ruby Flashyfur** and her friends weren't exactly team players. Anytime they got involved in an event, they wanted to do things their way.

"I hope not," Pam said. "That would stink

worse than rotten cheese!"

While the students waited to hear the news, Headmaster de Mousus gathered all the professors in the staff room. Time was *RUNNING OUT*, and they had to make a decision!

The headmaster cleared his throat. "My distinguished colleagues," he began. "There are exactly THREE MONTHS until the official ceremony, and we need to come up with a proper celebration."

The professors began to talk all at once.

"What about my idea?"

"No, mine is the best!"

The headmaster tapped his paw on the table. "Now, all of your proposals were good, but none of them were quite right," he said. "We need something . . . *mousetacular*!"

Across the table, Professor Margaret Rattcliff gave a little cough.

A professor of literature and creative writing, she was usually very quiet and kept to herself.

"The answer is obvious," she said. "William Squeakspeare, the great playwright, attended this academy many years ago. We should perform one of his *great works*!"

The headmaster's eyes lit up. "A *play*? That's just the thing!"

"This way, both students and teachers can be involved," said Professor Rattcliff. "We haven't had a play performed here since we shut down the theater department years ago. Mouseford Academy could use a little *drama* in these halls."

Headmaster de Mousus nodded. "It is exactly the *mousetacular* idea that we needed!"

AN AWKWARD SPY

All of the professors agreed that a William Squeakspeare play was the *perfect* idea for a celebration.

"This is a **wonderful** opportunity for the students," said Professor Mousilda Marblemouse. "The students who don't want to act can work behind the scenes. Others can handle publicity and make posters. Or they can —"

Before she could finish her sentence, a **loud noise** that sounded like an out-of-tune piano interrupted her.

PLINK! PLUNK! PLUNK! PLINK!

"What is going on?" asked Headmaster de Mousus.

Professor Marblemouse got up to investigate, and Professor Bartholomew Sparkle joined her. The **noise** was coming from a room next to the staff room that was used to store **musical instruments**.

The two professors *cautiously* approached the door and opened it. A streak of light lit up **Ruby Flashyfur**, who was hiding under a grand piano.

"What are you doing here?" asked Professor Sparkle.

Ruby quickly got to her feet. "I was, um . . . you see, I was . . . practicing the **piano**!"

The two teachers exchanged glances. They both knew Ruby well. It was clear that she wasn't there to practice the piano. She had been **eavesdropping**!

"I know what you're up to, Ruby," Professor Marblemouse said. "And I guess I understand. I know all of the students are **curious** to find out what the big celebration will be."

"But eavesdropping is still **wrong**," Professor Sparkle added.

Ruby tried to look **innocent**. "But I wasn't —"

"No excuses, Ruby," Professor Marblemouse said. "Now get to your room. And don't whisper a word about this to anyone. Not until the headmaster's **BIG ANNOUNCEMENT**."

"Oh, I promise," Ruby said, batting her eyelashes. But as soon as she got back to the dorm, she *BURST* into the room where her friends were eagerly waiting for her.

"You won't believe what I found out!" she squeaked.

SQUEAKSPEARE'S CHEESY PLAY

The next day, the school auditorium was buzzing with anticipation. Headmaster de Mousus was about to make a **BIG** announcement.

"I can't wait to find out what the celebration will be," Nicky said, practically bouncing in her seat.

Ruby walked past, her snout in the air as always. "Some of us in the know already know," she said mysteriously.

Pam frowned. "What does that mean?"

Paulina nudged her friend. "Sssh! The headmaster's about to speak."

Headmaster de Mousus cleared his throat. "Dear students, I am sure you are aware of the IMPORTANCE of this announcement," he began.

"Oh no," Nicky groaned. "It's another one of his **long** lectures!"

"Six hundred years is a major anniversary," the headmaster went on. "Therefore, it deserves a celebration worthy of . . . BLAH blah blah . . . one that will stand the test of . . . BLAH blah blah . . ."

He never stops talking!

"**NOOO!**" Nicky wailed, covering her ears with her paws, and her friends giggled. "Sssh!" Violet warned. "He'll hear you!"

The headmaster droned on. "BLaH blah blah . . . after much deliberation . . . BLaH blah blah . . . and an excellent suggestion by Professor Rattcliff . . . BLaH blah blah . . . we all agreed that we will put on a play!"

The chattering students suddenly became quiet. He had their attention.

"And not just any play," Professor de Mousus continued. "We will perform a work by Mouseford Academy's most FAMOUSE alumnus, William Squeakspeare!"

The audience burst into applause.

"And now Professor Rattcliff will give us more information about the performance," the headmaster announced.

"For the performance, we have chosen

Squeakspeare's greatest *play*," the professor said.

Everyone began to chatter. Which one would it be? *A Midsummer Night's Cheese? Much Ado About Cheddar? Rodent III?*

"This play tells the tale of two young friends from RIVAL cheese-making families," Professor Rattcliff continued. "One makes a fine blue cheese, and the other makes a tasty mozzarella. The CHEESE-CROSSED young rodents want to open their own cheese shop together, but their jealous families want to keep them apart."

The students let out a cheer. Everyone knew that play. . . .

"It's *Mouseo and Juliet!*" Professor Rattcliff announced, and the students started to talk excitedly.

Ruby raised her paw. "I know every line,

Professor," she **bragged**. "Mouseo, oh, Mouseo, wherefore art thou, Mouseo?"

"Please save it for the audition, Ruby," Professor Rattcliff said. "Tomorrow, we'll post an audition schedule in the main hall. Everyone is welcome to try out."

The students started to whoop and cheer again.

Headmaster de Mousus stood. "SETTLE DOWN, students. This meeting is over. Please proceed to your next class."

The young rodents RUSHED out of the auditorium, eager to start practicing for the tryouts.

THE COMPETITION HAD BEGUN!

THE AUDITIONS BEGIN!

The Thea Sisters stayed up **LATE** that night talking about the play. The next day, they walked together to the main hall to see the audition **ANNOUNCEMENT**. A crowd of **excited** students had already gathered around the board.

Auditions for the Mouseford Academy production of <u>Mouseo and Juliet</u> will be held this Saturday at 3 p.m. in the auditorium. All students interested in acting roles should attend.

Headmaster Octavius de Mousus

Paulina turned to her friends. "Are you all thinking of auditioning?" she asked.

"You bet!" said Nicky. "I've climbed MOUNTAINS and slept in the desert, but I've never had a lead in a play. Playing Juliet would be an awesome challenge."

"Juliet is such a BEAUTIFUL soul," Violet said. "Like a lilting concerto. I would love to win that role."

"I think Juliet is such a romantic part," added Colette. "I'd love to play her, and I'd wear a beautiful pink dress."

"Juliet is my favorite literary character," Paulina added. "I have STAGE FRIGHT, but I might try to get over my fear if I could play her."

"I'm just thinking about how proud Thea would be if I got the lead part!" Pam exclaimed.

"It's too bad we **all** can't play Juliet," Colette remarked.

The Thea Sisters got *quiet*. They knew that only one mouse could get the part of Juliet. Yet they all wanted it.

Paulina spoke up first. "I think I would be *happy* as long as one of us got the part," she said.

Pam nodded. "Me, too."

"We should make a **PACT**," Nicky suggested. "No matter what happens, we'll be happy for whomever gets it."

She held out her paw. Violet, Paulina, and Pam each put a paw on top of hers. Only Colette held back. She was staring *dreamily* into space.

"Hey, Coco?" Nicky asked. "What's up?"

"Sorry," Colette said, shaking her head. "I was *dreaming* about that pink dress."

She added her paw to the pile, and the friends made their pact.

"You know, we should get to the **library**," Violet suggested. "We need to find a copy of that play."

But when they got to the library, an **UNWELCOME SURPRISE** awaited.

REALLY, RUBY?

"How could there be none left?" Nicky asked the librarian. "There used to be a whole shelf of copies."

"I'm sorry," the librarian replied. "But two days ago, every copy of every one of Squeakspeare's plays was checked out."

"Hmm. **TWO DAYS AGO?**" Paulina asked. "And every single copy?"

"Maybe we can find some copies online," Violet suggested.

"But we'll lose practice time while we're waiting for them to arrive," Nicky said with a sigh.

The Thea Sisters sadly went back to Nicky and Paulina's room to figure something out.

"There's got to be a solution," Colette said. "I'm sure we could find someone to **share** their copy with us."

"That's just the thing," Nicky said. "I've **texted** everybody we know, and nobody has a copy."

Violet frowned. "That's **strange**. Then who took out all those books?"

Suddenly, the friends heard voices in the hall.

Oh, Mouseo!

"**That sounds like Ruby!**" Pam exclaimed.

"I think we should see what she's up to," Paulina said. "I have a feeling it's nothing good."

The Thea Sisters went into the hallway and found Ruby and her friends — the Ruby Crew — there. Each one of them held a copy of *Mouseo and Juliet*.

"Really, Ruby?" Nicky asked, folding her arms. "We should have known."

Ruby's eyes widened innocently. "What do you mean?"

Pam nodded toward the book in her paws. "How did you all get a copy of the play? The library has been out of books for two days — since before the play was even announced."

Ruby sniffed. "I don't know what you're talking about."

"I think you must have found out about the play early somehow," Paulina said quietly. "That's why yesterday you said you were 'in the know.'"

Ruby shrugged. "I still don't know what you're talking about," she **insisted**.

"That's not fair," Nicky said. "We should —"

Violet put a paw on her shoulder. "Don't WORRY about it. I think I have an idea."

They all went outside. Pam shook her head. "That Ruby!"

"Forget her," Violet said. "I was thinking— Headmaster de Mousus said the auditions were open to everyone. So I'm sure Professor Rattcliff has more **books** somewhere."

"**GREAT IDEA!**" Pam agreed.

They went right to the professor's office, and Violet explained that the library was out of books. (She left out their SUSPICIONS about Ruby. Focusing on the auditions was much more important.)

As she predicted, Professor Rattcliff was very helpful.

"DON'T WORRY," she assured them. "I had a feeling that Headmaster de Mousus would love the idea of doing the play, so I ordered enough copies for everyone last week. They should be here tomorrow."

"**AWESOME!**" said Nicky.

Then Professor Rattcliff opened a drawer in her desk. "Since I can see you are especially eager to practice, you may borrow my personal copy," she said, handing a book to Paulina.

"Thank you so much!" Violet exclaimed. "We'll take *good care* of it."

"Prepare yourselves well," the professor said. "A combination of **DEDICATION** and talent will get you far."

The friends thanked her and left her office.

"Can you believe that?" Pam asked. "I always thought she was the **strictest** professor. But she's being super-nice."

"I've always liked her," Paulina remarked. "She loves **books** as much as I do."

Nicky broke into a run. "Come on!" she yelled. "We need to tell everybody the **good news!**"

THE GECKOS

The Thea Sisters and the Ruby Crew weren't the only ones excited about trying out for the play. So were the members of the **Geckos**, the school's club for boy mice. They gathered in their meeting room on the second floor of the academy to practice.

Most students thought that **CRAIG** would get the part of Mouseo. He was handsome and charming, and he loved being the center of attention.

"That Romeo was a real tough guy, like me," Craig said, **puffing out** his chest. "I would be **perfect** for the part."

CRAIG

But Shen, the shyest rodent in the club, didn't agree. He knew the play well and thought that Mouseo was sweet and sensitive—a dreamer, just like him.

Shen thought he was perfect for the part. And he knew who would be his perfect Juliet — Pamela!

IF HE AND PAMELA GOT THE LEAD ROLES, HE WOULD FINALLY HAVE A CHANCE TO TALK TO HER....

"Shen? Wake up Shen!"

Shen awoke from his daydream to find Craig shaking his arm.

"Sorry, what?" SHEN asked, almost

dropping the **books** he was carrying.

"I was just saying that I should be the **OFFICIAL** member of the Geckos who tries out for Mouseo," Craig said. "Don't you agree, sleepyhead?"

Shen saw his dreams dissolve in front of

What do you think?

him. He wouldn't even get a chance to try out!

Then a rodent in the back of the room spoke up.

"You're not the only one with a chance, Craig," said Ryder Flashyfur.

All of the club members turned to look at him. Ryder, Ruby's brother, had the same red hair as his sister, but that's about as much as they had in common. MYSTERIOUS and quiet, Ryder mostly kept to himself. But whenever he spoke up, his magnetic personality got a lot of attention.

"Who else could play Mouseo?" Craig asked. "Not Shen, that's for sure."

Shen looked down at his feet.

"Well, you never know," Ryder said smoothly. "And I know I'll be trying out."

"You?" Craig asked with a snicker. "Up

on a stage? I thought you preferred hanging out in **DARK CORNERS**."

Ryder ignored him. "It's a really good play," he said with a shrug. "And that Mouseo is pretty **cool**."

"Ha! I don't believe you've even read the play," Craig said.

Ryder strode into the center of the room and began to recite lines from the play. Shen recognized them. They were from the famous balcony scene. In it, Mouseo tries to get Juliet to run away with him so they can start their own **CHEESE SHOP**.

The rodents in the room were quiet as Ryder said the lines. He was *perfect*! When he finished, Ryder left the room without a word.

"Wow," one of the club members said. "He was **GREAT**, wasn't he?"

Craig shrugged. "He was all right, I guess," he said. But to himself, he thought, *I hope he doesn't get the part. I want to play Mouseo, and I want Ruby to be my Juliet!*

Shen, on the other hand, couldn't help ADMIRING Ryder.

Now, that is the perfect Mouseo! Shen thought.

What's in a name?
That which we call cheddar
by any other name
would taste as yummy!

THE BIG DAY!

On the day of the auditions, the *Sun* looked like a big wheel of cheddar in the sky. Almost every student in the academy was in the hallway outside the auditorium, waiting to try out. Some were ANXIOUSLY pacing back and forth, and others were reciting lines **OUT LOUD**.

Paulina looked around. "There are quite a few roles in the play. A lot of students will get parts."

"But everyone wants to be either **Mouseo** or *Juliet*," Nicky pointed out.

Pamela grinned.

"YOU CAN SAY THAT AGAIN! THEY'VE ALL GOT THE THEATER BUG!"

"I am so NERVOUS," Colette said as she tapped her paw impatiently. "Waiting is the worst!"

Pamela, Paulina, and Violet were quietly reciting Juliet's lines. Ruby walked past them with her snout in the air, as always.

"I bet she's surprised to see that everybody has a copy of the play," Nicky whispered to Colette.

At that moment, the big clock in the hallway chimed three times.

BONG! BONG!
BONG!

"The auditions are starting!" someone shouted, and everyone RUSHED into the auditorium.

Inside, the CELEBRATION committee sat behind a large table, ready to hear the auditions. Professor Rattcliff, Professor Marblemouse, and Professor Sparkle would make the decisions, led by Headmaster de Mousus.

The students crowded into the auditorium, and a nervous silence filled the room. The headmaster stood up.

"Dearest students of Mouseford Academy, I now declare the auditions for the performance of *Mouseo and Juliet* officially open!" he announced, and the students broke into applause.

He pointed to a large vase on the table. "If you wish to audition, write your name on a piece of paper and place it in here," he instructed.

As the students began to scribble, he continued. "We will pull out the names from the vase one at a time," he explained. "That will determine the order of auditions and who goes FIRST."

"This seems more like a lottery than an audition," Pam whispered, and her friends all giggled.

"But it is a very honest method," Violet pointed out. "After all, whoever goes first will have an advantage. After hearing the same lines recited again and again, the judges will get tired by the end."

Colette gasped. "Oh no! What if I'm last? That would be terrible."

"Don't worry," Paulina soothed her. "After all, if you're the **BEST**, the judges will notice — even if you do go last."

Colette sighed. "Right! I just need a little **CONFIDENCE**, that's all." She scribbled her name on a piece of paper with her *pink* pen.

When they finished, the Thea Sisters walked up to the vase and dropped their names inside. Each one was thinking the same thing. *I hope I get the part of Juliet! But if I don't, I hope one of my friends gets it!*

¡T SMELLS LiKE SABOTAGE!

"One piece of paper per candidate," Headmaster de Mousus said loudly, as the **students** came up to drop their names in the vase. "Anyone discovered putting their name in more than once will be disqualified."

Ruby's ears perked up when she heard this.

A few minutes later, Alicia, a member of the Ruby Crew, spotted Ruby filling out several pieces of paper.

"What are you doing?" she asked **LOUDLY**.

"Sssh!" Ruby warned. "Do you want them to find out?"

"But the headmaster said you can't put in your name more than once," Alicia said.

The rest of the Ruby Crew, Zoe and Connie, approached them.

"What's going on?" they asked.

"Don't you get it?" Ruby said. "We can use this to our advantage."

"No, I don't get it," Alicia said, shaking her head.

"I'm not writing *our* names on the paper," Ruby explained impatiently. "I'm writing down the names of the Thea Sisters! So they'll be disqualified!"

Alicia's eyes lit up. "Genius!"

Connie grinned. "That is some impressive SABOTAGE."

The Ruby Crew **QUICKLY** got to work filling out as many **FAKE** sheets of paper as they could.

"Now none of the Thea Sisters will get to play Juliet," Ruby said. "In fact, none of them will get *any* part."

Then she and her crew **snuck** every piece of paper into the vase without anyone noticing.

WHO WILL PLAY MOUSEO?

While they waited for the audition schedule to be announced, the Thea Sisters went outside to get some FRESH AIR in the school's garden. The warm sun felt good on their fur, and the air smelled of flowers.

Nicky STRETCHED. "I'm getting stiff from sitting around waiting!"

Paulina nodded. "Me, too. Let's take a WALK."

"Good idea. I need to shake off some nervous ENERGY," Colette agreed.

Violet held back. "I'm going to stay here and go over my lines again."

Colette looked surprised. "But, Violet, you've repeated your lines a million times.

Plus, you're *AMAZING*!"

"Thanks," Violet said with a shy smile. Her friends nodded in agreement. Violet was *EXPRESSIVE* and sensitive when she read Juliet's lines.

"I'll stay here and give you a paw, Vi," Pamela offered.

So Pamela and Violet stayed in the *garden* while Colette, Nicky, and Paulina took a walk in the courtyard. Nicky noticed Ryder Flashyfur leaning against a column. She had always been a little curious about Ruby's shy brother.

"Let's go say hi," Nicky suggested.

As they approached Ryder, they noticed that he seemed to be *talking* to himself. Then Paulina figured it out.

"He's reciting lines," she said. "For Mouseo's part!"

"Interesting," Colette said *thoughtfully*. "I thought for sure that Craig would be the only member of the Geckos trying out."

"Craig?" asked Nicky.

"Well, he's the most OUTGOING," Colette said. "And Ryder usually likes to stay in the SHADOWS, you know?"

Come on!

Just then, Violet and Pamela caught up with them. Panting, Violet announced, **"The list is up!** Come on!"

The Thea Sisters *QUICKLY* ran back to the building to find out where they were on the audition schedule.

PAMELA

DÍSQUALÍFÍED?

A large group of curious heads **BOBBED** up and down in front of the list. The Thea Sisters waited their turn. But when they got to the list, they **discovered** that their names weren't on it!

They read it again and again in disbelief.

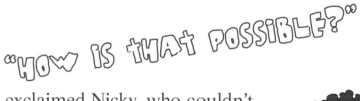

"HOW IS THAT POSSIBLE?"

cxclaimed Nicky, who couldn't believe her eyes. "Not a single one of us is on here!"

They were all SPEECHLESS for a moment. What

could have happened? Then Professor Rattcliff walked up to them.

"Come with me," she said in a whisper. "I'm afraid there is a problem."

The Thea Sisters looked at one another as they followed the professor up to the second floor. Something **TERRIBLE** was going on!

Professor Rattcliff led them to Headmaster de Mousus's **OFFICE**. He looked them up and down, and he seemed to be very annoyed.

"I am very disappointed in you students," he said. "When we counted up all the names, we discovered that your names appeared many times. The rules about this were very CLEAR!"

This news startled the Thea Sisters. Violet stepped forward to object.

"THAT CAN'T BE TRUE! WE DIDN'T DO IT!"

"That's not possible," whispered Paulina quietly.

"We followed the rules," protested Pam.

Professor Rattcliff interrupted. "I believe you," she said. "You have never misbehaved

since you have been at the academy, and I don't think you would start now."

The headmaster nodded. "We have gathered all of the **PAPERS** with your names on them. Let's see if we can FIGURE OUT what happened."

The Thea Sisters carefully examined the papers. They quickly noticed a very important detail.

"One of these names is in my *handwriting*," Pam said, "but the rest aren't. See?"

Looking at the papers, it was **CLEAR** that someone else had written the names of the Thea Sisters on the extra slips of paper.

The headmaster nodded. "You are right. These extra names were added by *someone else*!"

The Thea Sisters breathed a sigh of relief.

"Someone must have played a terrible **trick** on you," Professor Rattcliff said. "We'll conduct an investigation. Until then, I'll put your names at the bottom of the list."

"Thank you!" the friends said.

When they left the office, Nicky turned to the others. "Ruby has her 🐾🐾🐾🐾 all over this!" she said. "We should say something. Then *she'd* be disqualified."

"We don't have proof," Violet said. "Besides, I don't need to play games like Ruby does. If I get the part, I want it to be because I'm the best — not because someone else got disqualified!"

THEATER FEVER

The Thea Sisters made their way back to the *auditorium*. They passed by Craig as they entered.

"What are you doing here?" he asked. "I thought you were OFF THE LIST."

"That was a MISTAKE," Violet said. "We're back on it — at the bottom."

Craig shrugged. "It doesn't matter anyway. Ruby is so going to get the part of Juliet."

"Why is he so SURE about that?" Nicky wondered, as they walked off.

When they got inside, they saw that Headmaster de Mousus and the rest of the committee had returned as well.

"QUIET, everyone!" the headmaster announced. "I need the first five rodents on

the list to please line up by the stage."

The nervous students *QUICKLY* lined up. The rest of the students sat in the auditorium to watch as they waited to be called.

The auditions went by at a very fast pace. Many boy mice tried out for the part of Mouseo, and many girl mice tried out to be Juliet. They were all fine, but there was something MISSING.

"We need actors with a little more . . . spark!" Professor Rattcliff told the other judges.

But so far, nobody was quite right.

Then Craig's turn came. He put so much ENERGY into his performance that when he declared his love for Juliet, he pounded on the floorboards, breaking one of them.

Shen gave a sensitive performance, but he

was so nervous that he kept FORGETTING his lines.

Connie from the Ruby Crew was a little too **LOUD**, and Zoe was a little too *quiet*.

At the judges' table, Professor Marblemouse sighed. "I don't think we're going to find the perfect Mouseo and Juliet in this bunch!"

A DREAM AUDITION

Professor Rattcliff looked down at the list.

"Next up . . . **Ruby Flashyfur**," she called out.

The auditorium suddenly went quiet. Ruby swept down the aisle in a beautiful blue gown, just like Juliet would have worn. She looked stunning.

Even so, Ruby felt nervous. She tried to SHAKE OFF the feeling.

Why are they wasting time listening to these other actors? she thought.

I am the Juliet they're looking for!

Ruby held her head high as she made her grand entrance.

I was born for the stage, she reminded herself. *This is the moment I've been waiting for!*

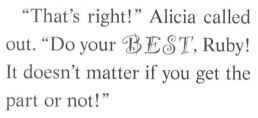, show them you're the best!" Connie yelled from her seat.

"That's right!" Alicia called out. "Do your *BEST*, Ruby! It doesn't matter if you get the part or not!"

Ruby stopped and scowled at her. The other members of the Ruby Crew shook their heads at Alicia.

"What did I say that was so wrong?" Alicia asked.

"It *does* matter if Ruby gets the part," said

Zoe. "She *has* to get the part!"

Ruby reached the stage and began to read her lines. Soon it was clear.

SHE WAS REALLY GOOD!

There was no denying it. Her performance was filled with real emotion. And she had

that "spark" the judges were looking for. They couldn't take their **EYES** off her.

"Now, *that's* a Juliet," said Professor Marblemouse.

Even Professor Rattcliff, who was usually very serious, let a **TEAR** fall from her eye.

"Just lovely," she said.

Headmaster de Mousus stood up. "Well then, we have found our Juliet!"

Luckily, Professor Sparkle came to the rescue of the Thea Sisters.

What feeling!

"To be fair, we should hear from all the students before we decide," he said.

The headmaster sighed. "Very well, then. Let's get this over with."

Colette was more nervous than ever. "There's no way any of us will beat Ruby!"

But Violet had a DETERMINED look in her eyes. "We'll see about that," she said.

"May the best mouse win!"

A THRILLING
AUDITION

"Colette! You're next," Professor Rattcliff called out.

Colette NERVOUSLY got onstage.

"You can do it, Colette!" the Thea Sisters cheered.

Colette took a deep breath. Then she recited her lines. While she declared her feelings for Mouseo, she did a pirouette, sighed, and clutched her paws together.

"Good, but maybe a little TOO MUCH feeling," Professor Marblemouse whispered to the others.

The rest of the Thea Sisters took their
turn. Nicky's performance was
ENERGETIC and **LIVELY**.

Pamela forgot most of her
lines, so she improvised instead.

"Hey, Mouseo, let's forget
about this cheese and go on a
TRIP around the world," she
quipped. But the judges didn't
seem to enjoy the new **twist**
on the old
classic.

Paulina was so
shy that she spoke all of
her lines in a whisper.
She was still good, though,
and everyone quieted down,
RIVETED, so they could
hear her.

"She's good, but no one would be able to HEAR her in the back rows," remarked Professor Sparkle.

Finally, it was Violet's turn. Any NERVOUSNESS she had vanished once she stepped onstage. She briefly closed her eyes and tried to imagine being on Juliet's balcony. She could almost feel the COOL BREEZE on her fur and hear the leaves rustling in the trees.

As she recited her lines, she transformed herself into Juliet. She took everyone in the auditorium with her on a trip to the ENCHANTED land created by William Squeakspeare.

When Violet finished, everyone applauded like crazy.

The judging committee began to whisper to one another.

"Ruby was **WONDERFUL**, but so was Violet," said Headmaster de Mousus.

Professor Rattcliff nodded. "Yes, they're both *perfect* for the part!"

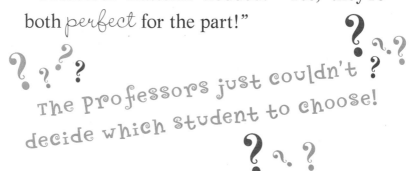

The professors just couldn't decide which student to choose!

Finally, the headmaster stood up and addressed the crowd.

"We are not ready yet to make any **final** decisions," he said. "Ruby and Violet, we would like to see each of you again here tomorrow at **one o'clock** for a second audition. After that, we will decide who will play the role of Juliet."

A murmur rose from the crowd. Violet and Ruby were both **SHOCKED**.

The auditions weren't over yet!

An Unexpected Mouseo

The students in the crowd were about to leave when the headmaster made an **ANNOUNCEMENT**.

"We almost forgot," he said. "There is one more name on the list: Ryder Flashyfur."

Ryder **CONFIDENTLY** strode onto the stage and began to recite his lines.

"I love you more than **CHEDDAR**. When I'm with you, there's nothing **BETTER**."

The professors and students all got quiet. Ryder was performing the part with his whole *heart* and soul.

"**WOW!**" exclaimed Craig loudly, nudging the rodent next to him. "Who knew Ryder had it in him?"

"Shhh!" the student hissed. *"I want to listen!"*

Everyone was completely MESMERIZED as Ryder finished his lines. It was pretty clear that he would get the part of **Mouseo**.

Headmaster de Mousus dismissed everybody. Craig walked up to Ryder.

"Well, it looks like I won't be playing Mouseo," he said. "But I hope your sister gets the part of Juliet. She was the **BEST**."

Ruby joined them. "Oh, I'll get the part," she said **CONFIDENTLY**.

Ryder raised an eyebrow. "How can you be so sure?"

"Because I'm the best, of course," Ruby replied with a wicked twinkle in her eye.

A MYSTERIOUS
INVITATION

Violet woke up **early** the next morning. Now that it was between her and Ruby for the part of Juliet, she wanted to get in as much **PRACTICE** as possible. Instead of waking her friends, she took her copy of *Mouseo and Juliet* and went to the *garden* to read her lines.

She wasn't the only one up early. Violet found Ruby near the fountain, wearing workout clothes and doing some stretching exercises.

Violet walked up to her. "Good luck today," she said.

Ruby snorted. "I don't need any *luck*!"

Then Craig jogged by. "I'm **rooting** for

you, Ruby!" he called out, and Ruby smiled.

I suppose a lot of students are rooting for Ruby, Violet thought. *But I can't let that distract me.* She found a *quiet* spot on a bench and began to go over her lines.

Hey, Violet!

"*Hey, Violet!* You're up early!"

Violet looked up to see Nicky waving at her. Her friend wore a tracksuit and was headed out for her morning *RUN*.

Violet left her book on the bench and went to meet her friend. "I wanted to get some **EXTRA** practice in," Violet explained.

"**GOOD!**" Nicky replied. "But don't overdo it. You were a NATURAL yesterday. Meet you in Colette's room before lunch, okay?"

Violet nodded. "See you later!"

She went back to the bench. When she picked up her book, a **NOTE** fell out. She picked it up and read it:

Dear Violet,
I thought maybe we could rehearse the parts of Mouseo and Juliet together. It's hard to concentrate at the school, so maybe we could meet at the observatory. How about 10?
I hope to see you there.
Bye,
Ryder

Violet was surprised. The **MYSTERIOUS** Ryder wanted to practice with her? They had never really even had a conversation before.

Still, she liked the idea. It would be easier to practice her lines with someone reading the lines of Mouseo. And Ryder was so **good**. . . .

She looked at her watch. It was **9:30**.

Why not? she decided. She had plenty of time to GO to the observatory, practice with Ryder, and then GET BACK in time for lunch with her friends and her audition.

She picked up her book and started **walking**, reciting lines softly to herself as she went.

CAUGHT IN A TRAP!

The astronomy observatory was built on top of a hill and was the highest point on Whale Island. From there, students could observe the sky and the STARS without being disturbed by the lights on the island. A large telescope stuck out from the dome-shaped building, pointing toward the sky.

Violet walked along the narrow path that traveled through Hawk Woods and continued up the hill. It felt good to walk in the fresh morning air, and the VIEW was beautiful.

On one side of the path, she could see the glittering blue ocean down below.

GREEN trees and plants grew on the other side. She heard wings flapping and turned to see a **FALCON** fly out of the trees.

From the corner of her eye, she saw a large **SHADOW** moving in the brush.

"Ryder?" she called out, but there was no answer.

Suddenly, a sparrow popped out of a bush and began to fly in circles around Violet.

"Oh, it was just you," she said, LAUGHING to herself. "I thought someone was there."

When Violet reached the observatory, she opened the large front door. On weekends, only the museum inside was open, and it was usually quiet and EMPTY — the perfect place to rehearse.

"Ryder?" Violet called out.

There was no reply.

"I'm here!" Violet said.

"**HERE** HERE HERE . . ."

her echo responded.

She looked at her watch.

It was **10:10**.

Ryder should have arrived by now.

Maybe he's running late, Violet thought. *Might as well wait.* She stepped toward a **MAP OF THE STARS** that hung on the wall. The map had always fascinated her, and she leaned in for a closer look.

A few seconds later, she thought she heard a **noise** outside. She turned just as the door shut loudly behind her.

"Oh no!" Violet cried. She *RAN* toward the door and pulled on the handle, but it wouldn't OPEN!

She pulled again, but it didn't **budge**. She was locked inside!

But how had the door closed? Violet wondered. A sudden *GUST OF WIND*? But it wasn't windy outside. . . .

It seemed really **strange**, but there was nothing she could do. Violet tried her cell phone, but she couldn't get a signal.

Her only hope was that Ryder would be there soon.

"**Ryder, where are you?**" she called out.

THE USUAL
SUSPECTS . . .

Back at Mouseford Academy, Connie, Zoe, and Alicia were chatting in the garden when Ruby ran up, still wearing her workout clothes.

"Hi," Connie said. "Where did you DISAPPEAR to? We looked everywhere for you."

"Yeah, we almost thought that Violet had locked you up somewhere because she was SCARED of having to face you today," added Zoe, and the other members of the Ruby Crew LAUGHED.

Ruby just shrugged. "She might be worried about me, but I'm not worried about her," she said BREEZILY.

Alicia sighed. "Wow, Ruby, I sure wish I had your **SELF-CONFIDENCE**!"

A little while later, the Thea Sisters were in Colette's room, ready to go to lunch — but Violet hadn't showed up.

"Has anyone **SEEN** her recently?" Colette asked.

"Not since early this morning," Nicky replied. "She was going over her lines. But she promised she'd meet us for lunch."

"And her audition is at one o'clock!" Pamela said WORRiedlY. "This isn't like her at all."

"We should see if she's still in the *garden*," Paulina suggested. "She's probably just still practicing."

The friends headed down to the garden, where they saw Ruby and her crew.

"Hey, Ruby, have you seen Violet?" Nicky asked.

"Why are you asking me?" Ruby **SNAPPED**. "I haven't done anything."

"What do you mean by that?" Pamela asked suspiciously.

"Oh, NOTHING, nothing," Ruby said, with a nervous laugh. "She's probably just off practicing somewhere."

Oh, nothing . . .

The big outdoor clock began to *chime* twelve times.

"Time for lunch, crew," Ruby told her friends, and they left without another word.

Nicky **SCANNED** the garden. "I don't see Violet anywhere."

"Lunch today is **EXTRA-CHEESE** pizza, and I'm not even hungry," said Pam. "I'm too worried about Violet."

Colette nodded. "I've been trying to text her, and she's not responding," she said. "I have a **strange** feeling that something terrible has happened to her!"

THE SEARCH
FOR VIOLET

"We'll do a SEARCH," Nicky suggested. "We'll start by asking if anyone has seen her. After we check the campus, we can move to other buildings on the island."

They went to the cafeteria first, in case Violet had gone there without them, but they didn't see her. They did **BUMP** into Craig, though.

"Hey," he said when he saw them. "Did you try the pizza? It's SUPER-CHEESY."

"No, we're **LOOKING** for Violet," Colette said. "We can't find her."

"She's probably hiding somewhere because she knows she can't beat Ruby," Craig said.

"Hey, that's not nice!" Pam cried. "First of all, Violet is just as good as Ruby. And second of all, she would never hide out like that."

Craig shrugged. "I wouldn't **waste time** looking for her. She'll turn up."

"You know what's **SUPER-CHEESY**? *Him,*" Pam muttered as he walked away.

The friends left the cafeteria and headed into the hallway. They saw **Ryder** about to turn a corner up ahead.

Pam suddenly **brightened**. "Hey, maybe he knows where Violet is," she said. "They might have been practicing together."

Paulina frowned. "That doesn't seem likely. He is Ruby's brother after all. But I guess we could ask."

"**Hey, Ryder!**" Colette called out loudly. "Have you seen Violet?"

Ryder shook his head. "No, sorry."

"It's just weird, because we can't find her anywhere, and the **SECOND AUDITION** is about to start soon," Paulina explained.

Ryder thought for a moment. "I'll help you look. Maybe we could **split up**. Colette and Nicky, you can look for her in the school. The rest of us can look outside."

"*Great idea!*" Nicky said. "Even if I did think of it first."

Pam gave Nicky a high five. "Let's make like a wheel of cheese and **roll**!"

A TiGER
in A CAGE!

For two hours, Violet had been pacing the floor of the observatory, trying to think of a way out. She had lost all hope that Ryder was coming.

She grew **ANGRIER** with each passing minute. "Ryder and his mysterious note!" she fumed. "If it weren't for him, I wouldn't be in this mess. *GRRRR!*"

She continued to walk back and forth, like a TIGER in a cage. Then she stopped and took a breath.

Violet, try to calm down and think, she told herself.

She scanned the room again. She pushed a chair up to the nearest window and stood on it. The window was sealed shut. And even if she could climb out, it was a long drop to the ground beneath.

What do I do now?

With a sigh, she climbed back down. She would **never** make it back to the academy in time for the audition.

Then she noticed a shaft of **sunlight**

coming through the window. It reflected off a TELESCOPE that had been put on display. An idea suddenly came to her.

"It's brilliant!"

A SHINING SOS!

While Violet tried to find a way to escape, Colette and Nicky **SEARCHED** all the school buildings for her. Pam, Paulina, and Ryder checked all the sports fields.

"No sign of her yet," said Pam with a **frown**. "I'm starting to get **really** worried."

"We'll find her soon," Ryder said, but his voice was a little unsure.

Paulina looked **THOUGHTFUL**. "Let's think. Where are some places on the island that Violet likes to go?"

"Well, there's the *garden*, but we've already checked there," Pam said.

"What about Kneecap River?" Paulina

asked. "I know she likes to sit by the water and sketch sometimes."

Pam nodded. "You're right! Let's go!"

Paulina, Pam, and Ryder RACED toward

the trail that led to the river. It was **12:30**, and the audition was just thirty minutes away. There was no **TIME** to lose.

When they got on the path, Ryder stopped to figure out the quickest route. That's when he saw a STRANGE FLASH of light on top of the hill.

It was coming from the observatory. But Ryder had **never** seen the observatory give off a light like that . . . unless . . .

"Pamela! Paulina!" he yelled.

The two mice turned around.

"What is it?" asked Paulina.

Ryder pointed to the observatory. "I think I may have figured out where Violet is," he said, his normally **calm** voice rising

with excitement. "See that FLASH OF LIGHT?"

Paulina nodded. "Yes."

"It's weird," Pam said. "I've never seen a **bright light** like that coming from the observatory before."

Ryder nodded. "Exactly. I think Violet must be in there . . ."

". . . and she's sending us a **signal**!" Paulina finished.

"Let me get my SUV," Pam said. "We'll head right up there!"

FiNALLY
FREE!

Pam tore up the road to the observatory, kicking up dirt behind her wheels. When they pulled up, they could hear Violet screaming inside.

"Heeeeeelp!
I'm locked in here!
Let me out!"

They **QUICKLY** got out of the SUV. "Calm down, Vi!" Pamela yelled, running to the door. "We're here now! We'll FREE you!"

Pam reached for the door and noticed that some long sticks of wood had been JAMMED under the handle.

"This is why Violet can't get out!" she realized.

She removed the sticks and pulled open the door. Violet *RUSHED OUT* and threw her arms around Pam and Paulina.

"I am so *happy* to see you guys!" she sighed. "Thanks! I got stuck in here some-how, and if you hadn't found me . . ."

Then she noticed Ryder standing behind them. "It's all your fault!" she said **FURIOUSLY**, stomping toward him. "What kind of trick was that? You invite me up here and then don't even show up?"

"Invited you up here?" Ryder asked in *shock*. "Me?"

Violet waved the **NOTE** she had received under his snout. "You sent me this note asking me to **practice** with you here!"

"I didn't write this, I swear," Ryder said.

"Then who did?" Violet asked.

"Um, Vi, you might want to figure this out later," Pam said. "We've got to get you to your audition — *FAST*!"

ALL'S WELL
THAT ENDS WELL!

"I still don't **UNDERSTAND**," Violet said as she climbed into the SUV. "Who would want to **lock** me in the observatory?"

"Someone who didn't want you to audition," Pam guessed. "Like **Ruby**."

"Or CRAIG," Paulina added. "He's really been rooting for Ruby to get the part."

When they got to the main hall, they spilled out and rushed to the auditorium. Nicky and Colette greeted Violet with **hugs**.

"The auditions are starting!" Nicky said.

When Violet entered, Ruby turned as PALE as a slice of mozzarella.

"But how did you get out . . . I mean . . ." she stammered.

Violet looked at her friends. **Ruby** had just given herself away. She was the one who had locked Violet in the observatory!

"I'm here now," Violet said calmly.

"May the best mouse win!"

Ruby auditioned first. She was so rattled by seeing Violet that she messed up her lines. When it was Violet's turn, she delivered her lines perfectly.

"We have made a decision," said Headmaster de Mousus. "The part of Juliet shall go to Violet!"

"Hooray!" shouted the Thea Sisters.

Over the next few weeks, all of the students worked together to put on the play. Colette helped design COSTUMES. Paulina and Nicky helped PAINT scenery. Pam worked with the lighting crew.

Even the Ruby Crew was busy. They created PROGRAMS for the night of the performance that told a summary of the story of *Mouseo and Juliet*. It wasn't the most glamorous job, but Ruby and her friends worked hard on it anyway.

Mouseo and Juliet
By William Squeakspeare

This play is set on Mouse Island in the 1500s. Juliet and Mouseo are teenaged rodents who belong to two rival cheese-making families. Juliet's family, the Ratulets, make a delicious blue cheese. Mouseo's family, the Montagues, make a delicious mozzarella. One day at a picnic, their lunches get mixed up. Juliet eats the mozzarella and Mouseo eats the blue cheese. They both realize what they've been missing all their lives.

One moonlit night, Mouseo visits Juliet, who talks to him from her balcony. He convinces her to run away with him so they can open their own cheese shop together. But when their plans are revealed, their families do anything they can to keep them apart.

BRAVO! ENCORE!

On opening night, spectators **crowded** the main hall. Colette, Nicky, Pam, and Paulina made sure they got **FRONT-ROW** seats. When the curtain opened, Violet spotted her friends right away.

Pamela stood up and started cheering.

"WAY TO GO, VIOLET!" YOU'RE THE BEST!"

Violet tried not to smile. The support of her friends meant so much to her.

Professor Rattcliff gave Pam a **severe** look.

"Sssh!" she scolded. "Be quiet!"

Once the crowd calmed down, the show began. The performers had rehearsed many times, and everything went smoothly. A few actors forgot their lines and improvised instead, but nobody noticed.

When Violet and Ryder did their scenes together, something magical happened. The whole audience was transported to a different place and time. You could practically smell the CHEESE in the air. . . .

When the final curtain fell, the audience burst into joyous applause. The Thea Sisters hugged one another. They were so happy for their friend!

Even Ruby applauded. She was jealous of Violet, and would have loved to get the applause instead — but she had to admit that Violet was really **great**. And she was happy for her brother, of course.

Afterward, everyone agreed on one thing — there really is something magical about the theater!

It was truly a night to remember!

Don't miss these exciting *Thea Sisters* adventures!

Thea Stilton and the
Dragon's Code

Thea Stilton and the
Mountain of Fire

Thea Stilton and the
Ghost of the Shipwre

Thea Stilton and the
Secret City

Thea Stilton and the
Mystery in Paris

Thea Stilton and the
Cherry Blossom Adventure

Thea Stilton and the
Star Castaways

Thea Stilton: Big Trou
in the Big Apple

Thea Stilton and the
Ice Treasure

Thea Stilton and the
Secret of the Old Castle

Thea Stilton and the
Blue Scarab Hunt

Thea Stilton and the
Prince's Emerald

Thea Stilton and the Myst
on the Orient Express

Thea Stilton and the
Dancing Shadows

Thea Stilton and the
Legend of the Fire
Flowers

Thea Stilton and the
Spanish Dance Mission

Thea Stilton and the
Journey to the Lion's Den

Thea Stilton and the
Great Tulip Heist

n't miss
y of my
umouse
ventures!

#1 Lost Treasure of the Emerald Eye

#2 The Curse of the Cheese Pyramid

#3 Cat and Mouse in a Haunted House

#4 I'm Too Fond of My Fur!

#5 Four Mice Deep in the Jungle

#6 Paws Off, Cheddarface!

#7 Red Pizzas for a Blue Count

#8 Attack of the Bandit Cats

#9 A Fabumouse Vacation for Geronimo

#10 All Because of a Cup of Coffee

#11 It's Halloween, You 'Fraidy Mouse!

#12 Merry Christmas, Geronimo!

#13 The Phantom of the Subway

#14 The Temple of the Ruby of Fire

#15 The Mona Mousa Code

#16 A Cheese-Colored Camper

#17 Watch Your Whiskers, Stilton!

#18 Shipwreck on the Pirate Islands

#19 My Name Is Stilton, Geronimo Stilton

#20 Surf's Up, Geronimo!

#21 The Wild, Wild West

#22 The Secret of Cacklefur Castle

A Christmas Tale

#23 Valentine's Day Disaster

#24 Field Trip to Niagara Falls

#25 The Search for Sunken Treasure

#26 The Mummy with No Name

#27 The Christmas Toy Factory

#28 Wedding Crasher

#29 Down and Out Down Under

#30 The Mouse Island Marathon

#31 The Mysterious Cheese Thief

Christmas Catastrophe

#32 Valley of the Giant Skeletons

#33 Geronimo and the Gold Medal Mystery

#34 Geronimo Stilton, Secret Agent

#35 A Very Merry Christmas

#36 Geronimo's Valentine

#37 The Race Across America

#38 A Fabumouse
School Adventure

#39 Singing
Sensation

#40 The Karate
Mouse

#41 Mighty
Mount
Kilimanjaro

#42 The Peculiar
Pumpkin Thief

#43 I'm Not a
Supermouse!

#44 The Giant
Diamond Robbery

#45 Save the
White Whale!

#46 The Haunted
Castle

#47 Run for the
Hills, Geronimo!

#48 The Mystery
in Venice

#49 The Way of
the Samurai

#50 This Hotel Is
Haunted

#51 The
Enormouse Pearl
Heist

#52 Mouse in
Space!

#53 Rumble in
the Jungle

#54 Get into
Gear, Stilton!

#55 The Golden
Statue Plot

#56 Flight of the
Red Bandit

The Hunt for the
Golden Book

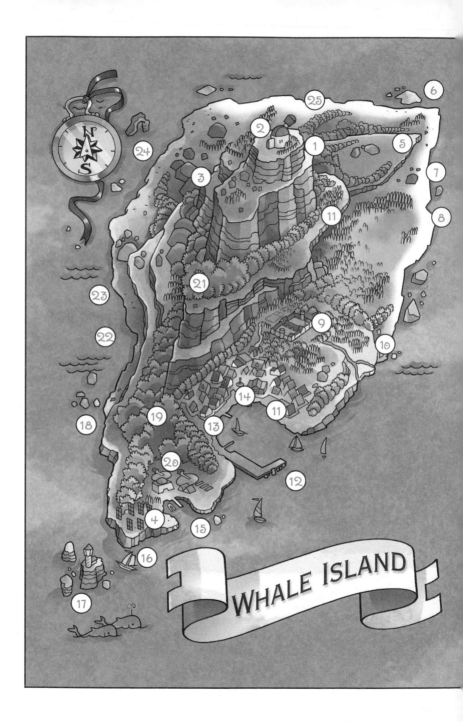

MAP OF WHALE ISLAND

1. Falcon Peak
2. Observatory
3. Mount Landslide
4. Solar Energy Plant
5. Ram Plain
6. Very Windy Point
7. Turtle Beach
8. Beachy Beach
9. Mouseford Academy
10. Kneecap River
11. Mariner's Inn
12. Port
13. Squid House
14. Town Square
15. Butterfly Bay
16. Mussel Point
17. Lighthouse Cliff
18. Pelican Cliff
19. Nightingale Woods
20. Marine Biology Lab
21. Hawk Woods
22. Windy Grotto
23. Seal Grotto
24. Seagulls Bay
25. Seashell Beach

THANKS FOR READING, AND GOOD-BYE UNTIL OUR NEXT ADVENTURE!

Thea Sisters